THE FALL OF

ICARUS

N.R. BATES

N.R. Bates

The Fall of Icarus: short stories/N.R. Bates

ISBN Number: 978-0-9931905-6-8 (mobi)

ISBN Number: 978-0-9931905-7-5 (epub)

ISBN Number: 978-0-9931905-8-2 (print):

This book is dedicated

to my wife, Margaret H.P. Best

ACKNOWLEDGEMENTS

I would like to thank the following. Margaret H.P. Best—without her support this collection of short stories would not exist, and for her patience and her reading and listening to drafts of this novel. S. J. Parkinson—I am truly grateful for his continued encouragement during the light and dark days of writing and publishing. Lynn McNamee at Red Adept Publishing (RAP), North Carolina, for her advice. Sarah Carleton at RAP for her patience, dedication, and patience with multiple edits of these short stories. Jason Anderson at Polgarus Studio, for his formatting of this book. In the cover design, the photograph of altocumulus is credited to Norikazu; while the human with wings logo is credited to Sergey Korkin—both on license from Shutterstock. All of you have my deep and grateful thanks. This collection of short stories was inspired in part by the painting, The Fall of Icarus, by Pablo Picasso.

1
THE ELEVATOR

The moving elevator carried me in its deliberate, ordinary manner until it jolted to a stop and, at the flicker of overhead light, lurched sideways in a purposeful but tremulous motion. I couldn't help but let out a stifled gasp, fearing the worst, as I instinctively reached out to the elevator wall to steady myself, and the cane I temporarily used clattered on the metal floor. The thud of its impact added to my surprise, and my other hand reached into the fabric of my back pocket where my cell phone nestled—in safety still.

"What is wrong with the lift?" I hastily thought,

slipping into British English. I often switched between words from both sides of the Atlantic Ocean without it being a willful, deliberate choice. "Mobile phone" would slip out in the US and "cellphone" in the UK, or "gas" and "petrol" would be reversed. The habit suited my name, Ianos. I was baptized after a mythical namesake, *Janus*, the god of doorways—the god of two faces, of the present and past, and of endings. The latter term—"of endings"—seemed the most appropriate at that moment.

I shared the elevator with a neat stack of bottles still tightly sealed in a covering of plastic, waiting to be released to join others somewhere within the building. The fragrance of warm bread, lying in a basket atop the bottles, filled the elevator. It was the sixth time I had taken the elevator, and its character had settled into the familiarity of memory. The first time I used the elevator, briefcase in one hand, cane in the other, and straps of my carry-on lightly weighted over my shoulders, I couldn't help but notice the size of its interior. It was a tiny elevator. It occurred to me that if it came to an unexpected stop, and the lights turned out, I could have reached out to touch its walls with the tips of my elbows, and the claw of claustrophobia would have risen up into my throat. I banished those momentary thoughts. The elevator was shabby and well used—comfortable in its worn state. Beyond that, it exuded a nondescript air, and it certainly did not betray any hidden aptitude.

The second time I used the elevator, I noticed it had a maximum occupancy of three people—specified in bold French on the fixed plate and, beneath it in smaller type, an embossed printed version in English, German, and Arabic. By the third time, the elevator and I had settled into a mutual trust.

The evening before, I had checked into the hotel close to the metro stop. I walked straight past the entrance of the hostelry, confidently sure of direction, and then, humbled not to have noticed it the first time, retraced my steps to find the unassuming way in. The hotel entrance lay nestled between a well-illuminated fruit and vegetable shop and a Brasserie. The former had an orderly arrangement of colourful produce, seemingly inured to exposure from the cold and drizzly air, and the latter had metal framing holding thick, plastic walls that contained a coterie of empty and occupied tables and seats of painted sepia and bronze, warmed by tall heaters. Both premises firmly extended their footprints across the pavement, establishing their right to existence on common ground. No wonder I'd missed the recessed entrance to the hotel the first time I passed.

It was my first business trip—so said the suit in the mirrored hallway of the lobby. The fracture in my knee had nearly healed, and the annoyance of its sharp healing had not stopped my travel. "*Bonsoir, Madame*" and all the words that followed were said in haltingly poor French. I had arrived a day late and, after agreeing to pay for an empty room from the night before, was invited to use the elevator. The elevator welcomed me: up to shower and sleep and then, hours later, down for breakfast. Up again to prepare myself for the meeting, down again to hand in the key, and up again to drop off my briefcase at the end of the day. After experiencing the tiny elevator, the tiny room did not surprise me—it was like a large closet but with everything in its place. A small television hung on the wall, and it showed nothing but Canal channels in French. The windows opened to my seated place on the side of the bed and let in the cold air and the street's illumination. Every so often, a metro train would pass quietly along the elevated track way above the street level. In one corner of the room, there was an enclosed bathroom with a shower, toilet, and sink that had been carved out of the bedroom's original dimensions. It had everything except a bidet. It was functional and utilitarian—just like the room of the house in Hammersmith that I shared with antipodeans on their one- or two-year-long ventures away from home—and I needed nothing more. Peering out of the hotel window, I had an extraordinary view of the illuminated Tour Eiffel over the rooftops. The skyline was set against the backdrop of night clouds that reflected diffuse light back towards the city below.

On my first morning in Paris, before I left to go down to breakfast, I hid the briefcase under the bed and the notebook under the mattress.

"*Bonjour, Madame. Merci, Madame,*" I said politely to the middle-aged woman who tended the Salle de Petit Déjeuner. The taste of morning baguette, salted butter, and sweet apricot jam seemed identical to my childhood memory, and I savoured their flavours. No other place I'd lived in or visited had the same character to its bread or its croissants. I sat alone as no other delegates to the meeting had chosen to stay at the same hotel.

Another jolt of the elevator reminded me of where I was—trapped inside an aberrant elevator. I must have been in the elevator for at least twenty seconds as it yawed up and down a little during its determined sideways motion. I even banged on the metal side of the lift in a weak attempt to let the outside world know that I was in difficulty. The duress had not reached a point where I felt I could reinforce my fists with a voice. Perhaps my voice would betray weakness in the echo within the lift, and this thought stopped me from calling out. Just as I was getting used to the motion, the deep whirring of the elevator ceased, and its doors opened.

A toupee of turf topping a bank of soil greeted me. The incongruity of the rural landscape momentarily stopped my breathing. But hearing the whirring of the doors as they initiated their closing, I clasped the doorframe of the elevator, and I lurched forward, eager to escape its confines. I mistimed my step, the ground being a foot beneath the floor of the lift. I found myself deep in a ditch, my shoes overtopped in an instant by cold brown waters and my hands and knees buried in the soft mud of the bank. I could not restrain my swearing—my suit was ruined. The soft clunk of the elevator doors came from behind me. I pushed myself upright and, after a long stare, surmised that the elevator had disappeared.

"What wonders."

I scrambled up the bank and stood amidst a narrow, grassy verge that surrounded a field of carrots and potatoes. I wiped the clumps of wet soil off my shoes and knelt to transfer as much of the bank as I'd gathered on my hands and fingers to the tall, reedy grasses and their florets. My shoes were ruined.

My hands brushed against a few abandoned discards of vegetables upturned from the field. I leaned forward to pick up a curly carrot dangling from its thick rosette of leaves. The field was slowly being ploughed and its harvest turned under. I watched an ancient tractor pass along, the chug of its exhaust drowning any other sound. The birds and animals scattered before the overturning soil. I felt hidden in the grasses and crouched as low as I could—with an overwhelming sense of strangeness and being out of place adding to the pull of gravity. The details of the man driving the tractor were obscured—just a cap and turned-up overcoat and arms that extended to a steering wheel. I watched further as the rabbits—or were they hares?—bounded around the field in confusion. One of them startled and froze in its tracks close by, our eyes meeting. After a brief twitch of its muzzle, it broke free from my enchantment and leapt across the ditch to disappear into the thick sedges of the adjacent field. My gaze followed the animal. A curtain of trees in the mid-distance, bounding the fields and hedgerows, did not allow me to see any farther.

It was not entirely a rural scene. The end of a row of tall buildings abutted the large field, with chimneys emitting thick trails of smoke. My cane had been abandoned to its fate within the elevator, and I limped carefully over the small hummocks of the field's verge towards habitation. I soon found myself in an alleyway and then discovered something extraordinary—a familiar street. A metro train quietly rattled past on its tracks above me. Perplexed, I retraced my steps across the glistening cobbles, but I could not find the field with its crop being ploughed under. I gave up and returned to familiarity. At the stop of traffic, I found myself back in the safety of the hotel's entrance.

"*Bonsoir, Monsieur*," the receptionist greeted. It was not the receptionist from the evening before. Her bright smile disarmed me, and I felt a loss for words with which to cry out and relate the strangeness of my recent experiences. She looked at me without a comment or trace of surprise in regard to the disarray of my suit and the streaks of dried mud on my face.

"Hallo… *Mademoiselle. Chambre onze…* eleven… *si'l vous plait.*" I could say no more as she passed the keys into my open hand.

The elevator was empty except for my cane, which leaned in the corner. I reclaimed it. Upwards the elevator travelled, without incident, and then I escaped to quickly walk along the hall to my room. I lay on the bed after a hot shower. My drying shoes, socks, and trousers gave off steam as they lay over the hot metal radiator, and I felt content to watch the vapours rise. I carefully washed the carrot, which I'd kept gripped in my other hand since I gathered it from the field. And I ate it. Its sweetness reminded me of my father's carefully tended harvests of long ago. I opened the window and placed the green rosette into the window box. I could not make sense of my recent experiences. I was unable to speak aloud to anyone else—as if the event itself wanted me to keep the adventure secret.

~~~

The second time it happened, I was on my way down to breakfast in the elevator. No one joined me, and I shared the space with a tall-wheeled trolley. A stop, a flicker of the overhead lighting, and the aberrant elevator repeated its wayward sideways motion—except that this time I remembered to look out of the elevator through the small, diamond-shaped peek hole in the door. Instead of the alternating pattern of floors and metal doors that would have passed by during its normal vertical motion, the elevator lifted up in an upward arc and then down again. It passed fields and woods then houses and taller, imposing buildings. The elevator slowly spun on its axis—like a wooden top at the end of its motion and close to toppling over—allowing me to view the outdoors.

I was more prepared than I had been the first time. When the doors of the elevator finally opened, I gingerly stepped down onto the pavement with cane in hand. Again, I felt the waft of air as the doors closed behind me. I turned around and could not feel anything with my raised hand where the mechanism should have been. I stood in a narrow alleyway. But I was not alone. A young man stood staring at me with paint canister in hand, and nearby, a scooter leaned up against the wall. We must have been close in age to each other.

"What do you want?"

"Nothing. *Rien.*" After a few moments, I added, "Do you mind me watching you paint?"

The young man shrugged his shoulders and turned to face the brick wall. He sprayed out the foundations of one letter and then another. He painted boldly with a surety of purpose and maturity. It was a *wildstyle* of graffiti. The letters were indecipherable but involved interlocking forms and connecting points. The artist used three colours—red, yellow, and blue—with the shadows of the letters sharply and skillfully painted in black. I could not understand the tag he used, and I was curious about the painting.

When he was close to completing his artwork, I asked, "What does it mean?"

"It means nothing. Why should this mean anything to you? Perhaps I don't want it to be deciphered." His face came close to mine.

I could feel his breath on my face. Perhaps I imagined it, but I could have sworn he smelt of anise and camphor, and the green colour of absinthe came to my mind. He finished his work and carefully packed his canisters and a stencil in his rucksack.

"I don't understand it," I called after the man after he'd lifted his rucksack over his shoulders and rode off slowly on his Vespa. He did not look back at me.

I left the drying paint in the alleyway and came out into the street. I remembered this arrondissement. The Musee d'Orsay stood solidly opposite me, and after I examined its architecture for a while, the twinkling of its lights drew me in. I pulled out the hand I had kept in my pocket since the lift had deposited me in the alleyway and, with it, my wallet. I would have happily paid the entrance fee but was prevented by the waving hand of an attendant bidding me to enter. I spent a couple of hours wandering, stopping and sitting under the massive arches and glass ceiling of the hall—its Beaux-Arts boldness still holding echoes of the trains that had once pulled to a stop in the station. Nowadays, the works of Seurat and Sisley inhabited the vast halls of the former railway station. The one work by the latter painter, a stream at the edge of the wood, I reimagined as a gentrified ditch next to the carrot field that now felt like a dream remembrance.

A young woman came and sat next to me, and we studied the paintings before us. She was elegantly dressed in burgundy and black, with a decorative scarf around her neck, and she clasped a notepad in her lap. The raising of her hand to draw back a loose lock of hair drew my attention. My attempt to unobtrusively examine her face failed, and she turned towards me, annoyed.

"What do you know of the painting?" She pointed at the painting in front of us with her eyes, fixed beneath a frown, set upon my own.

"I'm sorry. Very little."

"The bourgeoisie are all alike," she said with sarcasm. "They... *you* do not know much."

It was not a response I expected, and I couldn't keep from adjusting my jacket. I refrained from answering. She got up and disappeared in the gallery. I wondered if she was a student.

"I am so ignorant—in so many ways," I whispered towards the painting in front of me. I leaned forward and cupped my face in my hands as my elbows rested on my knees, and I let out a deep sigh.

Years before, when I was about fifteen, I'd imagined myself a student at the École des Beaux Arts—*un etudiant des arts*. Perhaps I would have sketched a nude or copied paintings or tried to capture some essence of life in the cafés abutting the streets. That romanticism evaporated when an art teacher said firmly to me, "You have no talent for this."

Finally, I got up from my torpor and sought out the museum shop, where I was surprised to find a poster of a painting by Jean-Michel Basquiat. I bought it quickly and then stumbled out of the museum and took a taxi to the hotel. I was annoyed. If I remembered my high school politics, I was now a member of the proletariat, a wage earner, not a member of the bourgeoisie. I felt very far from my alma mater of McGill University, where I'd studied under the gaze of Mont Royal. It was midday. I had almost forgotten the meeting.

"I forgot to give you my key," I said to the receptionist, and I turned and left the hotel.

~~~

The third time I was carried along with the aberrant

elevator, I shared it with a bicycle that had no rider. It was propped against the elevator wall, and I had to squeeze myself into the free space. As it moved, I steadied myself against a corner. I did not peek out of the window, being content to let the elevator transport me at its whim. In less than a minute, I found myself on the pavement outside the Notre Dame de Paris on the Île de la Cité. I knew the cathedral, and I felt a comfort that I'd been deposited so close to a familiar landmark. No one on the pavement next to me seemed surprised at the sudden appearance of a stranger in their midst. I looked up, knowing there were statues of chimera and gargoyles silently observing the throng of people below, but I could not see any from the steps of the cathedral.

After I entered, I sought out a rack with lighted candles that flickered at my approach. I felt a need to light a votive candle in remembrance of loved ones.

I felt the touch of a hand on my sleeve. "You look

like you are in need of making an offering." An elderly man proffered two candles and a box of matches. He spoke in French.

"*C'est vrai. Merci bien*," I replied.

I thought about all that I had lost—family members as well as my belief—as I placed one of the candles, now lit, into the rack before me. I stood for a moment in silence, but not in prayer as the elderly man who stood next to me might have expected. He intently watched me as if I were a supplicant. I crossed myself, not for my own benefit, but more for his—to assuage his evident suffering. I quickly fled from the cathedral after I noticed his hand—it reminded me of the hands of a priest I preferred not to remember. I felt guilty at my loss—and at my survival.

I found my way out and then to the river. I leaned over the stone parapet at the riverbank and calmed myself by studying the boats passing up and down the river. The few boats that passed me held tourists braving the elements on the top deck, while most peered out from the warmth within. I still clasped the second candle and placed it in my coat pocket. It was too cold to stand for long, even with the thick coat and turned-up collar that overlaid my suit. What a hub the river must have been at one time. It had been the lifeblood of the city for centuries, and the habitation and industry of Paris had spread far from the Seine. I returned to the hotel and used the lift without incident several times. I couldn't speak about the aberrant lift, fearing I might be thought mad. No, it was more than that. The experience muffled me entirely, preventing me from sharing my experiences.

~~~

The fourth time I found myself transported within the elevator, three other guests had squeezed themselves into the confinement on a lower floor. I nearly pointed out the proscription against occupancy of more than three people, but I didn't. The elevator began its journey, and I joined the others in a collective gasp as it stopped and then lurched sideways again.

No one said anything except the middle-aged man. "For fuck's sake—not again." The man had an angry accent I recognized as being from Arkansas. "Texarkana," he said in response to my inquiry.

"We're from Texarkana, on the Arkansas side," came the more kindly response from the man's wife.

I stared at the faces of each of my fellow travellers, as they did in turn with me. My gaze lingered on the eyes of the young woman, the copyist who had sat next to me at the museum. I caught the vague flicker of a smile in the narrowing of the outer canthi of her face. It was a relief to know that others had shared in the wanderings of the aberrant elevator.

The doors of the elevator opened, and the three of us followed the brusque Texarkanan out of the elevator. I recognized the restaurant. It was near the museum, and after a long, narrow corridor, it opened up into an inner courtyard with tables and chairs and an upper gallery.

"Bonsoir," welcomed the waitress who stood beside the elevator doors. "Please take a table wherever you would like. We opened tonight just for you."

"Let's sit together while I wait," insisted Eveline, the young woman from the museum.

We sat together for a little while drinking Framboise—*eau de vie*, the water of life—in two short champagne glasses. What did we discuss? The architecture of the museum and its exhibits, and Eveline's careful copying of the great masters—first in charcoal and then repeated in colour. I mostly listened and interjected my opinions when asked. We conspiratorially laughed at the Texarkanan, whose anger refused to dissipate. The man complained bitterly to the waitress about their planned dinner reservation at another restaurant, and his wife silently looked around her at the unoccupied galleries and the potted diminutive indoor palms that guarded several of the tables.

A young man entered the restaurant, and he strode confidently to our table. He nodded as Eveline stood up, and they kissed one another on both cheeks.

They whispered to each other, and I heard her call him, "Frérot." As I stood up, she briefly introduced me as another guest from the hotel, but she did not tell me the young man's name. We shook hands, politely. I wasn't sure if my face betrayed a hint of what I was feeling—jealousy.

"Do you want to come with us?" she asked me. "We'll eat elsewhere and then go to a club."

"I have an early flight home tomorrow," I said, making my excuses. She then kissed me on both cheeks and departed. I watched as they walked away, arms linked, and then they moved out of sight of the street door.

"How does it work," I asked the waitress after I had eaten bread and slices of Andouille sausage.

"What works?" she replied, puzzled.

"The elevator—*l'ascenseur.*"

"Oh that."

"How does it work?"

The waitress shook her head. "I don't know. It just does." She said this in such an emphatic manner that my hopes of further questioning—and more importantly, answers—evaporated.

"It's my great-grandfather's invention. He installed it in our hotel after the Liberation. It doesn't work so often nowadays. It's expensive to keep these vintage elevators operating, you know."

I was irritated and, on a whim, refused the main dish. I had wrapped the remainder of the sausage and bread in a paper napkin.

"I have to go," I said apologetically to the waitress, reinforcing *urgency* with a gesture to my cell phone. I left euros on the table to pay for the unserved dishes of the prix fixe I'd chosen and the gratuity, and walked out into the illuminated street. It was full of shoppers beneath lights strung between buildings and upon lampposts. I clumsily pushed my way along the pavement and came upon the familiar road with its elevated metro line. I walked back along the quieter side of the street, with my shoes and cane tip disturbing the puddles. The drizzle still fell.

A different receptionist sat behind the desk, and I waited in the lobby for the key. The doors of the elevator opened, and I peered in to see it occupied with a vase of roses and tulips tucked into the corner. A waft of air brought their scent out of the elevator into the lobby. I hesitated and let the doors close. I stared at the elevator call button in turmoil for a few moments and then turned away. I found the stairs and walked slowly up, with the run of the metal banister firm in my hand.

I left the hotel early, having taken my luggage down

the stairs. Step, step, bump and bump. In the pouring rain, it took forty minutes to reach the airport by taxi and three hours more to clear passenger screening before I could rest my back against the seat and close my eyes.

It is now, years later, when I sit at my desk in a nondescript cubicle, that these remembrances of the aberrant elevator come to mind. I am practiced at running well-established algorithms that spit out risk and hazard assessments that I pass on to others to balance risk and readjust premiums to allow for profit. Not for my own profit, I should add, except for my comfortable, well-paid job and housing allowance.

I ask myself, "Why the hell did I not take the elevator the fifth time?" as I think I can hear the whirring sounds of the aberrant elevator opening beside my chair.

2

THE FALL OF ICARUS

It was a tale I often read as an older child, filling me with a mixture of wonder and joy at the thought of being able to fly and dismay and bitter disappointment at its thudding outcome. I am reminded of the story, the *Fall of Icarus*, as I sit quietly in front of the painting by Pablo Picasso, commissioned for the United Nations back in 1957, thirty years before my birth. The construct of the painting before me comprises forty individual panels, mounted together on a concrete wall, around thirty feet high and thirty-five feet wide.

"I don't understand it," I say to my colleague, seated

beside me, as I gesture to the immense canvas.

"The painting, you mean?" As he explains, its meaning begins to make sense to me.

The painting depicts several bathers gathered at the sandy shores of the blue Mediterranean Sea. The bathers are naked and appear untroubled at the sight of a charred, blackened Icarus with damaged wings, falling towards the azure waters. The horror of Icarus, burned so deeply through flesh to the bones within, does not let me turn away my gaze.

As a child, I identified with Icarus—or, at least his attempt to fly. In the moments immediately after waking, when the potency of a flying dream still lingered, that reverie persuaded me that I could really fly. In dreams, I might be a small bird flying fast over the hedgerows and trees, or a lumbering human leviathan that floated without steerage or applied force above the tiled rooftop of the building I lived in. It didn't matter what form I took. The outcome remained always the same—I escaped the confines of architecture and upbringing until the harshness and reality of my waking state intruded. Icarus, before his fall, was my exemplar of escape.

In the myth of Icarus, he attempted to flee from his island prison alongside his father, who had constructed wings of wax and feather. I don't remember the cause of their flight, but it must have been overwhelming in its force for them to undertake such perilous action.

"Don't fly too close to the water as the humidity of the waves' breath will clog your wings," his father urged. "Don't fly too close to the sun. The intensity of its strength will melt the wax that holds your wings together. In both cases, you will fall to your death."

Icarus, of course, flew too close to the sun, and he tumbled downward as a consequence. That part of the story bitterly stung me as a child—Icarus captured and brought to earth. In later years, I abandoned the story, angered by its allegory. I couldn't stem the flooding viewpoint that Icarus was punished for complacency and, even worse, hubris. The praetors of overwhelming influence insisted that the middle was the only sensible path to follow, and not the extremes of thought. The cohort of my school days insisted that I follow a middle way—not too bright, not too foolish, and not too confident. I succumbed, and I did not excel in any way. Perhaps without realizing it, I followed this path as a means of real escape and not the imagining of escape by taking flight.

I reimagine the story of Icarus as I sit in front of the painted homily. I imagine that Icarus did not fall and that he did not suffer from extreme pride or over-confidence. Unbeknownst to his father, Icarus had looked out to sea from the cliffs of his island prison a few days before their planned escape. He listened to the warnings of his father, but he intuited a fuller understanding of his situation, one not given by his father: the middle path between the two fixed constraints of water and sun would not be successful. His father had the strength in his musculature to fly the middle path far enough to reach another island and escape. Icarus did not. The constraints of the physical world had conspired to doom him to death.

"What can I do?" he shouted out to the winds.

"You must fly up high at first, closer to the sun, and then conserve your energy to glide to your escape," came the response from the ether.

I imagine that Icarus contemplated this thought for a time and, once he had decided, returned to his wings that lay in his father's workshop. In secret, while his father slept, Icarus remixed the wax that bound his wings together with glue and then, once the wings were reassembled, hardened the wax bindings from the flame of a candle.

"I may not be able to alter the constraints of the world, but I can change my own limitations. I *cannot* fail in my ambition."

And with that, I see before me, in my mind's eye, Icarus flying close to the sun against the remonstrations of his praetor below. Higher and higher he flies, and the hardened wax does not fail. He then glides towards escape and lands safely upon the flats of a sandy shore, leaving his praetor far behind. In my retelling of the story, it is Icarus who escapes and his praetor who falls to the sea, exhausted of breath from the efforts of calling out for his son to take the middle path.

I am like Icarus *redux*. I am a survivor, after all. There have been times when I was forced to take a middle road. I am bright, not foolish too often, and definitely not over confident. But I have excelled and followed my own path to escape the imposed constraints on life—those of my own making and those of others. In the future, if I give birth to a boy, I will have already named him Icarus as symbol of escape.

3

THE GIRL

I seated myself on a bench in the small park, and I tried to remember who I truly was. I had purpose, and my mind was full of memories, but my name, oddly, escaped recollection. The pigeons gathered around my feet, and I set the bag of breadcrumbs in my lap. The birds were impatient, and I sparingly threw out the leftover pieces of morning baguette for them.

It was November, and the weak afternoon sun did not touch the bitterness of the cold air. Earlier, I had warmed myself with an espresso served at a bar-tabac close to the metro station before I wandered across the street to the park. I rebuffed the attentions of a middle-aged man at the bar with the wave of my hand—content with my own company—and I didn't need to frown with a mastered disdain. With an afternoon off, it felt good to have an aimless couple of hours to squander and inhale the dry, cold air whilst warmly clad in my favourite boots. A thick overcoat with fur lining and a scarf around my neck prevented any unwelcome ingress.

The garden park was no more than a quarter hectare in size, and the specimens of ash, beech, and oak clung to their last leaves. The small, copper-leafed maple had shed its cloak entirely. Beyond the metal railings of the square, the traffic in the avenue was sparse, but the cars, trucks, and mopeds from the distant square filled the park with a constant background. I loved this small oasis of summer greenness and winter barrenness, overlooked by apartment buildings stretching up six floors to the attics. They were not old buildings, but their architecture fit in with the other buildings on the broad boulevard. The vernacular of balustrades and modern ironwork window railings broke up the façades of brick and marble. In the summertime, I imagined the tall windows of the apartments being thrown open to catch the breeze and collect the afternoon sun or blocked with shutters. In the park, strangers passed by without noticing me, but a young mother with a pushchair and a toddler strapped by a cord to her wrist stopped to watch me feed the birds. The little boy stared at me, and he soon started to chatter and stamp his feet. I smiled back at him, but this did little to placate his mischievousness. Then, abruptly, he was pulled away along the gravel path and placed in his pushchair. I watch them leave the park. Based on their direction, I guessed that they were on their way to pick up an older sibling from the school close by.

An elderly couple, middle hands clasped and outer hands holding canes, ambled into the park and politely asked if they could share my seat.

"*D'accord*," I responded. I laughed along with them as they retrieved individual packets of bread for the birds, and we compared the feasts we had brought—my breadcrumbs down to the last dregs.

"It is so good to see a young woman who cares about the birds," the old man said to me, his face sparkling with brightness. "We come here often—for comfort and solace." He retreated into silence as his wife took over their conversation to inform me that they had fed the birds every single day since they retired.

"We've lived just around the corner for decades, and our children went to the academy towards the Rue Commerce. We often said we'd move to the countryside after Emil finished work, but we never had the courage to leave this neighbourhood." She gave a broad smile. Even with their difficulty walking, they remained an attractive couple, seemingly happy and content in their life. The lines of their faces could not hide how beautiful they both must have been in their youth—and that beauty had not disappeared.

"You are a storyteller, I see! I can tell from the way you hold your hands and how you observe people and your surroundings. The signs are all there."

"I am an archivist," I replied. "But you are correct. I record and write the stories of others. I love my work and listening to the histories of lives lived, irrespective of whether the tale is mundane, melancholic, or bucolic. I hear ordinary stories and sometimes a retelling of wonderful things—or memoirs that are profoundly disturbing."

"Will you tell us a story—a tale of wonderment?"

I nodded but added, "Are you not too cold to sit here and listen to me?"

"I'm fine. Emil, what about you?" The elderly woman cupped her gloved hands around his hands.

"I'm warm too—not too frail yet!" he said with a cheerful and defiant smile. "We prepare well for these icy winds from the east—from the farthest reaches of Siberia, I imagine."

I paused for a few moments to gather myself and glance at my companions. "It is a strange story—a dream, perhaps, and one that transcends belief. I will recall the tale as if she is me and I am her. I can't remember her real name, and I must call her simply *girl*." I emptied the last of the breadcrumbs onto the gravel, neatly folded the paper bag, and returned it to my coat pocket. I shuffled along the bench seat towards my companions, so that they might hear me better, and moistened my lips with the gloss I carried in the reaches of my handbag.

~~~

It is the tale of a girl who grew before her time. She lived in a gray building with tall echoing corridors that rebounded with talk and gossip as she quickly walked along with her friends.

"Do I need to take anything else but my clothes and books with me?" she asked one of the novitiates whom she'd befriended when she first arrived years before.

"No, that's it, *deary*! That's all you'll need. I can't believe how tall you are and how you have the burgeoning of a young woman. You have a room to yourself at last. Come along—let's get you settled."

It was about the time of her first menses, and because of her maturity, the girl was moved from the dormitory she'd shared with three other girls. The room was small and simply furnished, and she quickly felt comfortable in her new surroundings with her familiar things. Instead of the woods in the distance and a view of the coterie of houses at the end of the village, her window now looked out onto the courtyard where she could observe people's comings and goings. A few taller chimneys and rooftops were visible beyond the quadrangle, and at first she missed her view of the fields and the crows flying up from the soil—or from their roosts in the de-leafed trees. She filled her windowsill with books and the fragments of rocks she'd collected around the playing fields. Her four bears and two dolls sat on the bedside table, and her desk rapidly filled with papers, textbooks, and schoolwork she'd brought with her. She now had more freedom to visit the village shop, outside of the routine of school, schoolwork, chores, and mass on Friday and Sundays. As her gaze wandered to the statue and cross, she knew she was bereft of belief—choosing to follow the rituals out of respect for her friends and enemies alike.

Her bedroom door had a gift—a lock that needed a key from the outside to open. The girl sometimes felt the need to retreat, and she could read her books in solitude under the light of the window. A lock helped when she needed isolation and did not want to be disturbed.

Several weeks after she had moved into her new room, she felt herself falling asleep while fully clothed on top of her bed sheets. It was nighttime.

"Are you all right, child?" The voice spoke urgently. The girl felt lifted up and carried in strong arms but could not respond. A few moments later, she was righted, and her bare feet felt the firmness of the floor. She erupted into a coughing fit. The paroxysms lasted without end, and the novitiate lifted her again and carried her to the infirmary. They gave her water, and she sat up in a bed to cough, and eventually ease returned, allowing her to deeply breathe fresh air. She was told that one of the boiler vents had broken its seals and slowly seeped gas into her room. After the pipes and vents were repaired, the girl moved back into the comfort and safety of her room. But she always remembered to leave the upper panel of the window ajar.

Some days after the gas event, she noticed a strange tingling in her hands and feet while she lay in the darkness of night.

"I wonder if this is caused by my poisoning," she asked herself and then others. But an examination by the doctor from the village gave them no answers. The novitiates peered at her strangely but said nothing. When the girl thought about the tingling sensation, it occurred, and then, equally quickly, it would disappear when she wanted it to.

A week later, the girl felt a change within herself, and she locked herself in her room. She found a switch in her mind, and then it happened. She pushed her hands hard against the bed, and she rose off the sheets, slowly turning over until she gently bumped against the ceiling of her room. Her foot banged against the overhead light, and the metal lampshade clattered a little. Her sheets slipped off her and fell to the floor—but she did not fall.

"This is amazing," she gasped, but she stifled a further cry lest she disturb anyone. She coiled herself and pushed hard against the ceiling to tumble back towards the floor. She turned the switch off in her mind, and she erupted into laughter as she fell a few feet onto the wood planks of her floor.

~~~

I stopped my tale to examine the couple. "It's getting cold. Are you sure you want me to continue?"

"Yes. You are right—it is too cold. But we'd both like to hear the rest of the story." They affirmed this by nodding at each other. "Do you want to come to the warmth of our apartment? It's not far."

I agreed, and we left the birds and pigeons in the square to brave the cold, dry air spilling in from the east. Their apartment was not far—perhaps a hundred metres or so—and we walked slowly. I kept pace with their stiff walk and asked them about their children and grandchildren, and then about their work before retirement. Before long, we had taken the old metal elevator up to their floor.

"They installed these vintage elevators in the buildings—the architect had an eye for detail and history," Emil said.

The elevator opened to a tall hallway, and once through their door, we discarded our coats onto a wooden rack and our scarves and gloves on the ornate, marble-topped hall table. We slowly passed through a cluttered drawing room, with high ceilings and two tall windows at one end, and seated ourselves around a small kitchen table. The old man prepared coffee, and soon my hands warmed against the heat of a cup.

"Do you mind?" Francine asked me.

I shook my head and joined them in releasing the smoke of an unfiltered Gauloise cigarette towards the heights of the ceiling. "It's a habit I can't quite give up."

"Neither can we!"

"Shall I begin again?" I asked.

~~~

The girl got up from the floor and closed the curtains of her room. She tried again and found herself bouncing off the walls and ceiling. Soon, despite it being a small space in which to practice, she mastered the art of flying. She pushed herself off the floor, walls, or ceiling to provide a force for flight and discovered that shifting the weight of her arms or legs could move her in whatever direction she wanted. She was ecstatic.

"*Girl,* are you in there?" A fist banged against her door. She dropped to the floor almost immediately and stood up to open the door to an older girl—one of the prefects of the Upper Academy.

"I'm fine. I had a dream, and I fell out of my bed. I'm sorry if I disturbed you."

The older girl peered beyond her as if to discover whether there were other pupils in the room. Satisfied, the prefect slowly closed the door, and her footsteps along the hallway diminished to silence.

The girl kept her secret, locking her door first and

then concentrating on flying within the room. She grew fearful of discovery and the sense of restlessness that gnawed within. The girl longed to walk out into the woods—to separate herself from other pupils and to find the solitude to concentrate on flying upwards into the canopy of the trees. She imagined all sorts of animal life inhabiting the uppermost reaches of the tallest branches and leaves and squirrels and mice amongst the nests and roosts of birds. There would be small pools of rainwater in the hollows of the tree trunks high above the ground, containing frogs and tadpoles. She might recline for hours in a bed of leaves, safe from falling, examining the flow of clouds across the blue sky and the to-and-fro of active sparrows, thrushes, and crows.

But she kept remembering the proscription against her hidden talent—oft given in the chaff of a sermon and not in the core of its message. Only daemons and angels could fly! A mortal might risk her soul exhibiting such a gift or even thinking about such things. The girl had manifested the gift, and her talent was now beyond mere wishful thinking. She'd known of a former pupil who had flown up from the playing fields. The teachers had chased and caught her with hooked poles and nooses before bringing her to ground. It had ended tragically as the pupil had fallen upon the railings that lined the school. In a calm moment, the girl listened to a teacher recount the tragedy. Speaking in quiet tones, he described how he'd consoled the pupil as her life ebbed away.

"I need to talk with someone—to be able to confide in another," the girl said to herself when alone. "I cannot control my gift and my emotions." But she could not trust anyone.

It was a Friday. At first, the girl heard the mass with intent as she peered forward over the heads of others. She gazed at her fellow students in a row along the wooden bench and then at the fingers held on her lap.

The girl felt her restlessness intensify, and then she had a revelation. The words of the sermon had no meaning for her—she no longer felt under the constraints of strict dogma and *refinement* of behaviour. She gripped the edge of the bench, but it was too late—she was loosened from gravity.

A gasp arose in the auditorium as the girl floated upwards from the bench that had restrained her. The sermon ceased instantly, and absolute silence fell across the assembled. Then a bedlam of shouting and remonstration erupted. Two of the girl's friends jumped on the bench, but their hands and fingers could not reach far enough upwards. The girl floated towards the ceiling. Beneath her, several of the benches had overturned. The loudest shouting turned to anger, and violence emerged from the seeming placidity of a few seconds before.

~~~

"So, we get to the exciting part," Francine exclaimed. "Can I top up your cup with more coffee?"

I nodded and moistened my lips again. "It's the dry air… from Siberia."

The couple winked at me.

~~~

The swipe of a wooden bench, raised up by an irate collective of pupils, missed the girl. She didn't want to be swatted like a wasp, and with a full exhalation, she pushed herself into the eaves of the auditorium. The girl spotted her escape before the alarm could be raised, and she scrambled against the roof beams to then pull herself through the uppermost opening of the tall window. It was open for ventilation, and the ropes could not be pulled to close the mechanism quickly enough.

The girl laughed at the relief of her escape and the assortment of faces that pushed against the interior panes of the windows. She must have been at least forty feet above the ground. The ants came scurrying out of the auditorium's side entrance. She spied the ropes and nooses being prepared. The roof pitch was steep, and she gripped the metal runners that helped the snow exfoliate from the roof tiles during winter. The girl clambered up to the apex of the roof, and she sat for a moment to catch her breath—from exhilaration, not exercise. She was not going to be caught—unlike her much older sister, whom she barely remembered. It had been her sister who had died on the railings years before.

"I will not be caught," she shouted down defiantly to the few distant people who had spread out into the grounds around the building so as to catch a better view of the wayward girl.

What was she going to do now? She could barely contain her excitement. She was at the point of no return or calming herself and climbing in through the bell tower to face the consequences of her actions. Standing up at first to get her balance, she then confidently took a few steps towards the bell tower. She stopped and stared at two men who shouted at her as they gripped the arches of the tower's small, coved ceiling. They tried to reach out to her.

The girl shook her head, turned, ran along the ridgeline, and launched herself into the air. The ground beneath her feet opened up, and she seemed to gain speed away from the auditorium and the disturbed ant nest below.

She looked wistfully at the canopy of soft leaves and branches that passed below her—she'd not have the opportunity or time to redolently lie for a few hours under bright sunshine, in the nest of the tallest trees, and contemplate the world. A few of the people below started their cars, and the girl caught occasional sight of her pursuers through the trees. The canopy of the trees gave way to the open fields and coppiced fragments of woodland. A thought would bring a change in direction or a wobble up or down or sideways, and her flight gathered pace. Soon the flat valley that held the broad, silvery meanders of the river and its oxbow lakes gave way to hills and fewer signs of habitation. The air grew cooler, but the girl did not shiver. The enchantment of her flight filled her with wonder, and she knew she had made the right decision. She felt pulled along in a purposeful direction, and she spied the snows and ice in the mountains that resisted the warmth of summer.

The girl waved at the people in the few villages she passed over. They did not wave back except for a few curious children who appeared beyond the supervision of their guardians. She must have been a few hundred feet above the ground, and she felt safe from the nooses of adults.

A large boom echoed above the hills at a higher elevation, and the girl spotted the metallic reflection of two jet planes in the distance. She did not know their purpose but intuited that they might decide to shoot her down—such was their menace. But a low cloud enveloped her, and tiny droplets began to form on her skin. She was warm and the cloud cold, and rain droplets condensed. The girl felt the bitter cold of the mountain air as she flew ever higher, but the chill did not penetrate her thin frock. The light grew dimmer, and she found it difficult to breathe. Her eyes grew heavy, and she fell asleep.

~~~

"That's not the end of the story." I paused to stub out my cigarette and take a sip of coffee. "Just in case you are wondering."

~~~

The girl awoke, and her eyes opened to a blackness of sky that was filled with stars. Her hands were filled with the touch of stalks, and she sat up to find herself in a field of long grass of mottled green and brown. She heard voices—the sound of children laughing—and looked about her to see an occupied play set not too far away. The girl stood up. She felt perplexed by the daylight colours of the landscape and the coruscation of the stars in the integument above. There was no blue sky—no sky of any kind, no clouds or transition of deep blue at the horizon to muted pale blue directly above.

"I have no idea who I am," she whispered. She no longer had the appearance of a girl at the cusp of womanhood but was a woman dressed in a blue blouse and gray skirt.

The playing fields gave way to a village, and she wandered along its main path. The village was filled with people who greeted her warmly as if they knew her. A few of the villagers were playing pétanque—*la boule*—with the metal balls thudding onto the sandy floor, or sitting outdoors, drinking coffee. The girl heard loud arguments about philosophy, the universe, planets, stars, and galaxies. The girl, now as a woman, asked them if they knew her.

"Of course, I know you, *girl*," one middle-aged man replied.

"So, you are back, then? You have too much interest in them—the people. Sit for a while and have some coffee."

The girl nodded, and she sat. Soon, she sipped from a warm cup of espresso. She felt content to watch a game of chess being played out in front of her and listen to the exchange of conversations from those around her.

"You'll find the answers to your questions at the end of the lane," one of the villagers said to her.

"Thank you." The girl got up and passed several cottages of the village to a lane. She ambled along the footway and smelt the fragrances of the maquis. She recognized the shrubs and trees of the holm oaks, strawberry tree, juniper, sage, and myrtle. Soon, she came upon a larger building with an elaborate portico. There was no use resisting, and she entered. It was a library.

Several people smiled at her inside the immense hall, and they directed her to the back stacks filled with books. As the girl peeked around the corner, another woman—dressed in a blue skirt and gray blouse—gasped. It was the girl's sister.

"We always had the gift, you and I." The older woman—full of tears—embraced the girl. "Welcome home."

The girl and her sister sat at a table and shared the mysteries that the library held. The older woman reached over to the girl and ran a hand through her hair. "I missed seeing you grow up. We need to keep filling it—the library. You'll have to return again to gather the stories of humans, and then we'll fill the pages some more."

~~~

"That's the end of my story. It is all I have at the moment," I said, feeling exhausted and brushing a strand of hair back in place. "I am like the girl. Sometimes, I forget my name as if I'm always searching for it."

"I know it. We know it," the elderly woman said softly. "We know you so well. Eventually you'll remember your true name."

Francine reached out with a hand and passed it through the long locks of my hair. She spoke up.

"No one can change our natures or our gifts or our interests. I missed seeing you grow up again. But at least the three of us will have time to recollect together. You will have plenty of time—the rest of this life—to gather new stories before you leave again to fill the pages of other books."

I stood up and, at their beckoning, went to the window of their apartment. I saw the garden park below me, but at the same time, I saw a parallel image—a shadow—of another park filled with children and a village surrounded by maquis with the integument containing the stars above.

BY THE SAME AUTHOR

AT THE SHARP END OF LIGHTNING

(Book One of the Oceanlight Series)

THE GATHERING PLACES

(Book Two of the Oceanlight Series)

www.ingramcontent.com/pod-product-compliance
Lightning Source LLC
Chambersburg PA
CBHW020319150626
46552CB00022B/2974